The Man
and the Serpent

One day, a little Boy was walking down the village road. He was happily enjoying the scenery around him.

Now, by mistake, the Boy stepped on a Snake's tail!

The Snake gave out a loud cry. He got very angry and bit the Boy on his toe.

The Boy cried in pain and soon died. His father came running, hearing his cry.

The Man saw the Snake's bite mark on his son's toe and became very angry.

He brought his axe from the house and went towards the Snake. Then, he cut off the Snake's tail.

Now, the Man's cows and sheep were grazing in the field. The Snake wanted to teach the Man a lesson.

He also wanted to take revenge from the Man. In his anger, he bit the cows and the sheep.

All the cows and the sheep died. The Man became very sad and started thinking.

He thought, 'We cannot keep on harming each other. I will try and be friends with the Snake.'

The Man decided that he would offer a hand of friendship to the Snake by giving him some gifts.

He took some honey and food as gifts. He felt it would please the Snake.

The Man said to the Snake, "We both have hurt each other. Let us be friends now."

The Snake said, "Take back your gifts. You can never forget your son and I can never forget my tail."

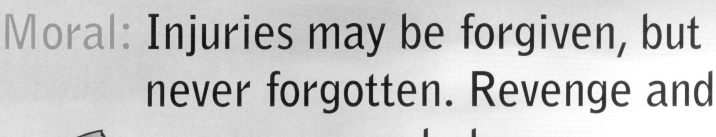

Moral: Injuries may be forgiven, but never forgotten. Revenge and anger never help.

Keywords

mistake   angry   brought

lesson   harming   friendship   forget